THE MYSTERY OF THE ORPHAN TRAIN

created by
GERTRUDE CHANDLER WARNER

Illustrated by Robert Papp

Albert Whitman & Company
Chicago, Illinois

The Boxcar Children Mysteries

Contents

THE MYSTERY OF THE ORPHAN TRAIN

CHAPTER 1

The Great Ethan Cape

"It's stuck!" cried six-year-old Benny. His round face was red from tugging at the zipper on his suitcase. "It won't budge an inch."

"Oh, Benny!" said twelve-year-old Jessie, coming into the room. She shook her head and laughed. "You're taking too much!"

Benny grinned at his older sister. "I think I packed too many socks."

As Jessie lifted the lid of the suitcase, several shiny red apples tumbled out onto the bed. "What on earth . . . ?"

Benny shrugged. "We might get hungry."

Jessie couldn't help smiling at this. Benny was famous for his appetite. The youngest Alden was always hungry.

"Don't worry, Benny," Jessie said as she tossed more apples onto the bed. "There'll be plenty to eat at Kate's bed and breakfast."

"What's a bed and breakfast?" Benny wanted to know.

"It's like a hotel," Jessie explained. "Tourists get a cozy bed, then breakfast in the morning."

Grandfather was traveling to Kansas on business, and Henry, Jessie, Violet, and Benny were going along. Grandfather's good friend, Kate Crawford, had invited the children to stay with her. Kate owned a big Victorian house called Wiggin Place. She rented out rooms during the summer.

"You can't be sure we'll find a mystery on this trip, Benny."

"But, Jessie, mysteries are always coming our way," Benny reminded her. "Right, Violet?"

"That's for sure, Benny," said ten-year-old Violet, who had just come into the room with Watch, the family dog. "We seem to find them wherever we go."

Nobody could argue with that. The Alden children loved mysteries, and together they'd managed to solve quite a few.

"What are you hiding there, Violet?" Henry asked curiously.

Violet pulled her hand out from behind her back. "Ta-daah!" She held up Benny's cracked pink cup, the one he'd found when they lived in the boxcar.

"Thanks, Violet," said Benny. The youngest Alden almost always took his special cup with him on trips. "I thought I packed it already."

After their parents died, the four Alden children had run away. When they discovered an abandoned boxcar in the woods, they made it their home. Then their grandfather, James Alden, found them and brought them to live with him in his big white house in Greenfield. He even gave the boxcar a special place in the backyard.

The Aldens often used the boxcar as a club-house.

As Jessie tucked Benny's cup into a corner of the suitcase, Watch gave a little whimper.

"Uh-oh," said Benny. "I think Watch wants to come with us."

"Sorry, Watch." Henry scratched the dog behind his ears. "Kate doesn't allow animals at Wiggin Place."

Violet gave Watch a hug. "Mrs. McGregor will take good care of you while we're gone." Mrs. McGregor was their house-keeper.

"We'll be back before you know it, Watch," Benny said in the middle of a yawn.

"I think we all need a good night's sleep," said Jessie, who often acted like a mother to her younger brother and sister.

"I'll second that!" Henry said, and the others nodded. They couldn't wait to set off on their next adventure.

* * * *

"Wiggin Place is just outside the town of Chillwire," Grandfather told the children as he drove the rental car along the highway from the airport. "We should have you there in time for dinner, Benny." He smiled at his youngest grandson through the rearview mirror.

"I'm all for that!" said Benny.

Violet, who had been gazing quietly out the window, suddenly spoke up. "I think I'm going to like Kansas," she said. "The countryside is so pretty."

"I was thinking the same thing," said Jessie.

"Kansas is a good place to visit," said Grandfather. "Of course, it's famous for its tall wheat and sunflowers, but it's also a great place to hunt for fossils."

"Fossils?" Henry, who was sitting up front beside Grandfather, raised an eyebrow.

Grandfather nodded. "They say this whole state was once covered by an inland sea. Folks are always finding the imprint of sea creatures on rocks," he said. "Sea creatures from long ago."

Benny put in, "I know something else about Kansas."

"What's that, Benny?" asked Henry.

Benny broke into a big grin. "This is where Dorothy lived!"

"Dorothy?" Grandfather looked puzzled.

Benny nodded. "Dorothy in *The Wizard of Oz*."

"Oh, that's right!" said Jessie. "In the story, Dorothy's a little girl from Kansas and one day she—"

"Gets swept away to the land of Oz in a tornado," continued Violet.

"With her little dog, Toto," Henry added.

"And they follow the Yellow Brick Road to the Emerald City," Benny finished, with a smile on his face.

"Right you are!" said Grandfather. "As a matter of fact, the playhouse in Chillwire puts on a performance of *The Wizard of Oz* every summer. It draws a lot of tourists into town."

"That must be good for local business," guessed Henry.

Grandfather nodded. "Kate's bed and breakfast is usually booked solid right through the summer. But then," he added, turning off the highway, "Wiggin Place has always been popular with tourists. You see, it has its own claim to fame."

They all looked at their grandfather in surprise.

"Claim to fame?" echoed Henry.

"What do you mean?" Jessie asked.

"Ethan Cape once stayed there."

"Oh!" Violet put one hand over her mouth in surprise. "Are you serious, Grandfather? Did the great Ethan Cape really stay at Wiggin Place?" Grandfather nodded.

Benny wrinkled his forehead. "Who's Ethan Cape?"

"He was a famous photographer, Benny," explained Henry.

"Didn't he take pictures of movie stars?" Jessie asked.

Violet nodded, her eyes shining. "And kings and queens!"

As they entered the little town of Chill-wire, Grandfather slowed to a stop to wait for a light to change. "Ethan Cape pretty much photographed all the prominent people of his day," he told them. "He left behind a wonderful record of the past."

"They say he was the best photographer who ever lived—a genius!" Violet knew a lot about photography. She always took her camera along when they went on vacations. "I was just reading about Ethan Cape. He was born in 1870. Nobody knows much about his childhood. His early life is a real mystery. But they do know he started taking pictures when he was a teenager. In fact, he wasn't much older than Henry at the time."

"Ethan Cape's photographs are worth a fortune these days," said Grandfather, pulling away as the light turned green. "I know Kate's turned down many offers for the photograph of her grandmother."

Violet blinked in disbelief. "You mean—"

"Yes, Kate has an original photograph taken by Ethan Cape." Grandfather grinned.

"Wow!" Violet's eyes were huge.

"I don't get it," said Benny. "Was

Kate's grandmother famous?"

"I was just wondering about that, too," added Henry.

"That's the strange thing. Kate's grandmother, Sally Crawford, lived her whole life in Kansas. From what I've been told, she was loved by family and friends, but she certainly wasn't famous." Grandfather shook his head in bewilderment. "And yet . . ."

"And yet what, Grandfather?" asked Violet.

"And yet Ethan Cape traveled all the way from New York just to photograph her."

"That's kind of strange, don't you think?" said Jessie.

"It sure is," agreed Grandfather. "And you know what else?"

They all looked at their grandfather expectantly. "What?"

"They say Ethan Cape had never even met Sally Crawford."

"But . . . why would a famous photographer travel all the way to Kansas to take a picture of an ordinary person he'd never even met?" Jessie wanted to know.

"That's a good question, Jessie," said Grandfather. "And it's a mystery to this very day."

Benny sat up straight and clapped his hands. "See, I told you we'd find a mystery in Kansas!"

Grandfather smiled at his youngest grandson. "I'm afraid that's one that may never be solved, Benny. Ethan Cape died many years ago."

Benny didn't seem a bit bothered by this. "We're very good detectives, Grandfather."

"True enough, Benny." Grandfather chuckled. "True enough."

CHAPTER 2

Wiggin Place

"Has Kate ever tried solving the mystery, Grandfather?" Jessie wondered as they left the little town of Chillwire behind.

"Oh, she's tried to figure it out, Jessie, but I think she gave up on it a long time ago. Kate puts all her energy—and her money—into restoring the old house. You see, she wants it to look the way it did in the olden days, when her grandmother grew up there. Actually, that's the reason Kate started the bed and breakfast," Grandfather told them as he turned onto a quiet country road. "She needed the extra money to fund her project."

"It must be a lot of work," Violet said thoughtfully, "taking care of a big house filled with guests."

"Well, Kate hires someone to help out during the summer months," explained Grandfather. "I don't think she could do it alone."

As they came to a white house with honey-colored trim around the windows and a peaked roof, Grandfather pulled into the driveway. A large sign on the front lawn read, "Wiggin Place—Bed and Breakfast."

"We're here!" cried Benny. "And look, there's even a pond in the front yard!"

"What a great place to cool off." Henry sounded just as excited as his little brother.

As they piled out of the car, Jessie looked around and said, "That must be Kate."

A woman with gray streaks in her dark hair was waving a hand high in the air as she hurried down the porch steps. Grandfather gave his good friend a hug.

"Kate, how do you manage to look younger every time I see you?" he asked.

"Never mind your flattery, James," said Kate, with a twinkle in her eye. Then she turned her attention to the children. "I can't believe I finally get to meet your wonderful family."

Grandfather smiled proudly as he introduced Henry, Jessie, Violet, and Benny to Kate Crawford.

"It's very nice to meet you," Jessie said politely, speaking for them all.

"I feel as if I know you already," Kate told them, as she slipped her hands into the pockets of a dress splashed with sunflowers. "Your grandfather has told me all about your wonderful adventures. And just between us," she added, "this place could use a little excitement."

At that, Grandfather had to laugh. "Kate, there's never a dull moment with my grandchildren around."

"Well, I'm glad to hear that!" Kate's laughter was warm and bubbly.

Grandfather lifted the suitcases from the

trunk of the car. Then he looked at his watch. "I don't like rushing away, but I do have a business dinner to attend."

Kate smiled. "Plenty of time to visit when you get back, James."

Grandfather gave each of his grandchildren a hug. "I shouldn't be more than a few days," he told them. Then with a cheery honk of the horn, he drove away.

The children waved good-bye, then followed Kate up the porch steps.

"You can unpack before dinner," Kate said.

"Oh, we can eat first if you want," offered Benny. "If dinner's ready, I mean."

"Benny loves to eat," Henry explained.

Kate laughed. "Then we'll make a good team, Benny. It just so happens, I love to cook!"

"Oh, look!" Something had suddenly caught Violet's eye. The others followed her gaze to a bronze plaque hanging beside the front door. The inscription on the plaque read: ETHAN CAPE ONCE STAYED HERE.

"We're very proud of our famous visitor," said Kate, a smile in her voice. "Of course, I was just a young girl when Ethan Cape photographed my grandmother."

Violet's eyes widened. "Oh! You mean—"

Kate nodded as they went inside. "Yes, I met the great Ethan Cape just a few months before he died. Of course, at the time I was pretty young," she added. "I didn't know he was famous until I'd grown up."

Jessie knew Violet was too shy to say anything, so she spoke up for her. "Violet's a photographer, too," she informed Kate as they headed for the staircase.

"Topnotch," Henry added. And Benny nodded.

"Oh?" Kate's eyebrows rose.

Violet's face got pink. "I still have a lot to learn," she said. "But . . . I would love to see the photograph."

Kate looked puzzled, but only for a moment. "Oh, you mean my grandmother's photograph," she said with a slow smile. "I'll be happy to show it to you after dinner, Violet."

Upstairs, Kate opened the door to a pretty room with rose-covered wallpaper and a four-poster bed that was just right for Jessie and Violet. Across the hall, a room with twin beds and blue-striped wallpaper was waiting for Henry and Benny.

"If you need anything at all, don't hesitate to speak up," Kate was saying. Then she turned her attention to a middle-aged man coming along the hallway. "Oh, Professor Brewer! Come and meet our new arrivals."

The professor, who had a newspaper tucked under one arm, was very tall, with a little gray hair around a bald spot. As Kate introduced the Aldens, Henry reached out to shake hands. But the man looked away, turning to Kate.

"What's the meaning of this?" he demanded. "There was nothing in your brochure about a pack of noisy kids running all over the place."

Henry and Jessie exchanged a look. Why was the professor so unfriendly?

Kate's smile disappeared for a second.

"Now, Professor, you're getting all worked up about nothing. The Aldens are wonderful children and I expect—"

"I expect peace and quiet!" the professor broke in sharply. Then he hurried away, leaving the Aldens to stare after him.

Henry let out a low whistle. "What was that all about?"

"I don't think the professor likes us very much," Benny said in a small voice.

"I'm sure he likes you just fine, Benny," Kate assured the youngest Alden. "The professor's a bit of a loner, that's all. I tried asking him a few questions when he first arrived. But he got very uncomfortable. He doesn't seem to like talking about himself." With a little shrug, she headed for the stairs. "Come down as soon as you finish unpacking," she called back to them.

The children couldn't help wondering if the professor would be any friendlier at dinner.

CHAPTER 3

Sally's Secret

It didn't take the Aldens long to unpack. In no time at all, they were following the wonderful cooking smells down the stairs to the kitchen.

As they stood in the doorway, they noticed a young woman standing by the stove with her back to them. Her blond hair hung in one long braid. She must have felt someone was behind her because she suddenly whirled around to face the children. A piece of paper fluttered to the floor. In a flash, she snatched it up and shoved it into her apron pocket. She looked as though they'd caught her in the middle of something she wanted to keep secret.

"I didn't realize anyone was here," she said. "I was, um, just checking out a . . . a grocery list."

Jessie couldn't help wondering if there was more to it than that. But she said only, "I'm sorry if we startled you."

Pulling herself together quickly, the attractive young woman smiled. "You must be the Aldens."

"Yes. I'm Jessie, and here are Henry, Benny, and Violet." Jessie motioned to her brothers and sister.

"And I'm Lindsay Lowe."

"Hi, Lindsay," said Benny. "Do you work here?"

"Kate hired me to help out for the summer," Lindsay told him, nodding as she tucked a loose strand of hair behind her ear.

"Can we give you a hand with anything?" offered Henry.

"Thanks, Henry, but everything's ready. Why don't we head for the dining room?"

A few minutes later, the children were sitting at a long table with Lindsay, Kate, and the professor. Jessie was just wondering about the two empty places when a young couple came into the room.

Kate quickly introduced the Aldens to her guests, Josh and Vanessa Mavin. Josh was a slight young man with curly dark hair and brown eyes. Vanessa was tall and slim, with reddish-brown hair and a splash of freckles on her nose.

"Have you seen any of the sights yet, kids?" Josh asked, after everyone had said hello.

Henry passed the mashed potatoes to Violet. "No, but we're hoping to get over to Dodge City."

"Grandfather said he'd take us," added Benny. He helped himself to a pork chop.

Kate nodded. "Yes, that's something you must see. Dodge City was once the Cowboy Capital of the World, you know."

Josh turned to his wife. "Now, that might be fun to check out."

Vanessa was pulling a biscuit apart. "I'm

not all that interested in cowboys," she said in a bored voice. "I'd much rather browse through antique stores."

Josh shrugged a little as he lifted green beans onto his plate.

"Kate knows all there is to know about antiques," Lindsay put in, looking fondly at her employer. "She's a real expert on the subject."

"Oh?" Vanessa looked over at Kate.

Kate shook her head. "I'm not really an expert, but I have—"

"What an interesting piece of jewelry!" Vanessa broke in. "Is that necklace an antique? It certainly looks old." Everyone followed Vanessa's gaze to the bluebird charm that hung from a gold chain around Kate's neck.

"Depends on what you call old," said Kate. "This necklace belonged to my grandmother. The funny thing is, she could never remember how she came by it. But she loved it all the same."

"It really is beautiful," Jessie said admiringly.

Violet nodded. "I've never seen anything like it."

"Neither have I." Vanessa carefully buttered each half of her biscuit, then ate two mouthfuls. "About how old do you think it is?"

Kate lifted her shoulders in a shrug. "I really have no idea."

"But it must be an antique," insisted Vanessa.

"Yes—I suppose," Kate said.

"Do you think it was passed down through the family?" pursued Vanessa.

Kate laughed a little. "Vanessa, there's no point in asking me all these questions. As I said, my grandmother couldn't remember who gave it to her. All I know is that she loved it, and always wore it on special occasions. In fact, she was wearing this necklace when Ethan Cape photographed her."

The professor, who had been staring glumly at his plate, suddenly looked up. For a long moment he fixed his gaze on Kate's necklace.

"Yes, yes, of course," he said at last, more to himself than anyone else. "That's the necklace in the photograph."

"Oh, have you seen it, Professor?" Violet asked shyly. "The original photograph taken by Ethan Cape, I mean."

The professor gave Violet a funny look. "Why do you ask?" he replied sharply.

"No reason, really," said Violet in surprise. "I just thought—"

The professor broke in before she could finish. "I have no interest in photography—or in Ethan Cape."

Everyone seemed surprised by Professor Brewer's harsh tone. Jessie caught Henry's eye. Why was Kate's guest so upset?

There was a strained silence until Lindsay spoke up. "You must see *The Wizard of Oz* while you're here, kids," she said, changing the subject. "I caught a performance last week and really enjoyed it."

Jessie was about to say something, but Vanessa spoke first.

"How much?" she asked, turning to Kate. She propped her knife on the edge of her plate. "Just name your price."

Kate wrinkled her forehead. "Are you talking about tickets to the play, Vanessa?"

"No, no, no!" Vanessa waved her hand in a frustrated way. "I'm talking about your necklace. I've taken quite a fancy to it."

Kate's hand closed over the bluebird charm. "I'm afraid it's not for sale."

"Oh, come now!" Vanessa rolled her eyes. "Let's cut to the chase, shall we? Everything has a price tag."

"No, Vanessa. You are quite wrong." Kate shook her head. "Everything does *not* have a price tag."

"But—" began Vanessa.

"Let it go," Josh told his wife through tightened lips.

At that, Vanessa backed off.

"Can you believe it?" Lindsay said later as the Aldens helped her clear the plates from the table. "Vanessa has such a nerve."

"She sure wanted Kate's necklace," said Benny, gathering up the napkins. "I wonder why."

"Vanessa wants everything she sees,"

stated Lindsay, who seemed to be getting more annoyed by the minute. "She's from a wealthy family, you know. From what I gather, she's used to getting whatever she wants." Lindsay paused to tighten the lid on the salt shaker. "Josh is a high school teacher. I'm afraid Vanessa's not used to living on a budget."

"It must be quite a change for her," said Violet, who never liked to think badly of people. "She probably needs time to get used to her new life."

"I suppose you're right," Lindsay said, backing down a little.

After helping with the dishes, the Aldens went looking for Kate. They found her in the front room, reading a book. She looked over and smiled when the children came through the doorway.

"Come and make yourselves comfortable," she said, setting her book aside.

Jessie and Benny joined her on the sofa while Henry sat in the rocking chair nearby. Violet couldn't resist settling into a lavender chair with padded arms. Purple was

Violet's favorite color, and she almost always wore something purple or violet.

"There it is, Violet," said Kate. She pointed to the picture that hung above the fireplace. "The great Ethan Cape himself took that photograph of my grandmother, Sally Crawford."

From inside an oval frame, a lady with snow-white hair and gentle eyes smiled down at them. Around her neck she wore a bluebird charm on a gold chain.

"What a wonderful picture," said Violet.

Kate agreed. "Ethan Cape was a brilliant photographer. He managed to capture my grandmother's inner beauty."

Jessie nodded. "You can see the kindness in her eyes."

"Everyone loved Sally Crawford, Jessie," said Kate. She paused to take a sip of coffee. "Sadly, she died a few weeks after that photograph was taken."

The Aldens looked at one another in surprise. "What happened, Kate?" Henry asked.

"My grandmother's health took a turn for

the worse, Henry." A shadow seemed to fall over Kate's face.

"Oh!" Jessie cried. "How sad."

"Yes, it was sad. But Sally Crawford died peacefully, surrounded by loved ones. Nobody can ask for more than that." Kate let out a long sigh. "What's really sad is that she never had a chance to reveal her secret."

"Secret?" Benny echoed in surprise.

"Yes, my grandmother was making plans to get the entire family together. She said she had a secret to reveal—a secret that had been kept hidden too long."

Nobody said anything for a moment. Then Benny spoke up. "You're not supposed to tell secrets," he said.

This made Henry smile a little. Benny was famous for not keeping secrets. "It's okay if it's a secret about yourself," he told his little brother.

Violet had been wondering about something. "Do you think the secret had anything to do with Ethan Cape?"

"It's possible, Violet," admitted Kate. "But not very likely. After all, Ethan Cape had never stepped foot in this house until he arrived to photograph my grandmother. Ethan Cape and Sally Crawford had never met before that day." Leaning back against a cushion, she let out a long sigh. "I doubt we'll ever know the truth. I'm afraid my grandmother took her secret to the grave with her."

The Aldens looked at one another. Was Grandfather right? Was this one mystery that might never be solved?

CHAPTER 4

A Hidden Message

"What a beautiful garden," Jessie said. The other Aldens agreed as they helped Kate gather flowers the next morning.

Kate looked pleased. "Thank you, Jessie. My guests often help out with the weeding. They find it relaxing." She added some daisies to the basket over her arm. "Of course, my younger guests prefer to swim in the pond or play in the jungle."

This caught Benny's attention. "Jungle?"

"Oh—that's the name my grandmother

gave to the woods over there." Kate twisted around and pointed. "When she was growing up, she'd pretend it was filled with lions and tigers and elephants. Sally often lived in a world of make-believe. You see, she never had any brothers or sisters."

Just then a doorbell sounded inside the house. A moment later, the back door flew open and Lindsay called out, "The truck's pulling into the driveway, Kate."

"I'll be right there!" Kate quickly tugged off her garden gloves. "Come and see it, kids!" she said, before rushing away.

Henry, Jessie, Violet, and Benny hurried after Kate. They watched curiously as two delivery men carried a dusty old desk into the front room.

"There's a spot for it right over here," Kate directed the men. "No, no. A little more to the left . . . more . . . more. Yes, that's it!"

As the delivery men went on their way, Kate clasped her hands. "My great-grandfather's walnut desk! And look, those are the original white china knobs on the drawers!" she added. "I can't believe the desk is back where it belongs. Of course, I'm still on the lookout for the matching chair. But I'll track it down."

When Kate paused to catch her breath, Henry said, "What do you mean about tracking it down, Kate?"

"The chair was sold at auction years ago, Henry. So was the old desk . . . a sideboard . . . some tables and chairs." Kate threw up her hands. "Oh, the list goes on and on."

The children looked at one another in surprise. "Why was the furniture sold?" asked Violet.

Kate answered, "I'm afraid my grandfather was a bit reckless when it came to money. Just after he married my grandmother, he lost a small fortune on the stock market. The bills were piling up, so . . ."

"The furniture was sold," finished Benny.

Kate nodded, sighing. "It was a sad day for my grandmother. But I've managed to track most of the furniture down and buy it back." She looked over at the Aldens. "Do you know where I found that desk? In a workshop!" she said, answering her own question. "The drawers were filled with garden tools."

"That would explain why it's so—" Jessie stopped herself in mid-sentence.

Kate laughed. "You can say it, Jessie— that desk is definitely a mess! I'll cover it with a sheet until I have time to give it a good waxing."

"Maybe we could lend a hand," volunteered Henry.

"Of course," agreed Jessie. Benny and Violet nodded.

Kate looked surprised—and pleased. "Are you sure? It's a big job."

"We like big jobs," said Benny.

Violet asked, "When can we start?"

"Right now, if you like," Kate said. "I'll get the rags and a can of furniture wax." Then she hurried away.

In no time at all, the four Alden children were hard at work. While they rubbed the wood to a shine, they talked about Sally Crawford's mysterious secret.

"I don't get it," said Benny, scratching his head.

"What don't you get?" asked Jessie.

Benny looked at them. "Why did Sally want to tell a secret if she'd kept it hidden for so long?"

"You got me!" said Henry, wiping out a grimy drawer.

"Maybe Sally just found out about it herself," Jessie put in.

"From Ethan Cape," guessed Violet, still thinking there was a connection between the famous photographer and Sally Crawford's secret.

"You might be right, Violet," Jessie told her. "But there's no way of knowing for sure."

"We'll get to the bottom of it," insisted Benny as he rubbed a china knob. "Right, Henry?"

Henry didn't answer.

"Henry?" Jessie asked. "Is anything wrong?"

Henry still didn't answer. He was busy patting all around the inside of a drawer.

Finally, he looked up and said, "Speaking of getting to the bottom of things, I think this drawer might have a false bottom."

"Oh, you mean a secret compartment?" Violet asked in surprise. "Is that what you're saying, Henry?"

"I'm not sure," Henry answered as everyone gathered round. "Let me try something."

They others held their breath as Henry slipped a finger into a knothole, then pulled up gently on the bottom of the drawer. Lifting it away, he said, "There's something underneath!"

"What is it?" Jessie asked in a hushed voice.

Henry reached into the secret compartment and removed a folded piece of paper, yellowed with age. As he silently read the note printed in black ink, his eyes widened and he gasped.

"What is it, Henry?" Violet wanted to know. "Don't keep us in suspense."

"It's some kind of message addressed to Sally Crawford," Henry said.

Everyone was staring at Henry. "Read it, okay?" Benny said.

Henry nodded. Then he read,

> *Where leopards get spotted*
> *a clue will appear.*
> *Just take a look under*
> *the little dog's ear.*

Benny made a face. "That sure is weird."

"I wonder who wrote it?" added Jessie.

"Thane Pace," Henry answered. "At least, that's how it's signed."

"Who was he, do you think?" wondered Violet.

"Maybe Kate knows," suggested Benny, already halfway to the door, with the others close behind.

It took them a while, but they finally spotted their friend coming up the front steps, letters in one hand, a rolled-up newspaper in the other.

"Oh—have you been trying to find me?" Kate asked.

"Did you know about the secret compartment?" asked Benny, who always got right to the point. "The one in the old desk?"

"Why, no," she said, sinking down into a porch chair. "This is the first I've heard of it."

Jessie said, "Well, guess what?"

"There's a false bottom in one of the drawers," Benny blurted out.

Henry added, "We found a note somebody wrote to Sally."

"Somebody by the name of Thane Pace," put in Violet.

Kate looked around at them, stunned. "Did you say . . . Thane Pace?"

Nodding, Henry handed her the note. As Kate read the strange message, the Aldens pulled the chairs closer and sat down.

"This is an amazing find." Kate shot the children a grateful glance. "A note from Thane Pace—written to my grandmother when she was just a little girl!" She shook her head in disbelief.

"But . . . who was Thane Pace?" asked Benny.

"He was the teenage boy who saved

my grandmother's life."

The children were so surprised by Kate's words they were speechless.

"My grandmother wasn't much older than Benny that winter," Kate said in a quiet voice. "She was skating all alone on the pond out front when it happened."

Henry gave Kate a questioning look. "When what happened?"

"The ice broke and Sally fell through—into the icy water."

"Oh, no!" Violet cried, horrified.

"What happened then?" Benny asked breathlessly.

"To make a long story short," said Kate, "a teenage boy, who happened to be walking along the road at the time, heard Sally's cries for help. At great risk to his own life, Thane Pace pulled my grandmother from the icy water."

Henry let out a low whistle. "What a brave thing to do."

For a few moments, no one spoke. Then Jessie asked, "Was he a neighbor? Thane Pace, I mean."

Kate shook her head. "No, he wasn't from around here. According to my grandmother, he lived some distance away. He'd left home to search for his sister."

"His sister?" Henry repeated, not understanding. "Was she lost?"

"I should explain," said Kate. "The thing is, Thane Pace and his sister came out to Kansas together on the Orphan Train. Thane was about ten years old at the time, and his sister was just a baby."

The Aldens were instantly curious. "What's an Orphan Train?" asked Benny.

"It was a train that brought orphans out west long ago. A group of people called the Children's Aid Society believed children who had no parents would have a better chance living on farms than on the streets of New York."

"Oh," said Violet, catching on. "Then Thane and his sister came out to Kansas to find a new family."

"Exactly," Kate said, nodding. "But sometimes a family wanted one child, not two."

"Oh, Kate!" cried Jessie. "You can't mean that . . . that . . ." It was too horrible to think about.

"I'm afraid it's true, Jessie," said Kate. "Thane was adopted by one family, and his baby sister by another."

The four Aldens stared at Kate in disbelief. Finally, Benny said, "We were orphans, too. Only, Grandfather wanted all of us to live with him."

"Even Watch," added Henry.

"There's nothing your grandfather values more than family," Kate said quietly. "But I guess that was true for Thane, too. He never forgot his baby sister. When he was old enough, he set out to find her."

"And did he?" Henry wanted to know. "Find her, I mean."

"Nobody knows, Henry," answered Kate. "Sally never heard from Thane again after her father—my great-grandfather—chased him away."

"What . . . ?" Henry could hardly believe his ears. "Why would her father chase him away? Thane saved Sally's life, didn't he?"

Kate sighed. "Apparently some money went missing."

Benny's eyebrows shot up. "Missing?"

"After Thane had been staying here for a few weeks, my great-grandfather accused him of theft."

Violet shook her head in disbelief. She couldn't imagine a hero like Thane Pace stooping to petty crime. That did not seem possible. But then, why else would Sally's father chase him away?

"I guess that's why this note was kept from Sally," Kate concluded. "If they thought it was from a thief, I mean."

"Maybe Thane put the note in the desk himself," offered Henry.

Kate thought about this. "Yes, I guess it's possible," she said at last. "If he knew about the secret compartment, that is."

"Did your great-grandfather have any proof that Thane stole the money?" Jessie wondered.

"I'm not sure, Jessie," Kate admitted. "It happened so long ago."

"I bet he didn't do it," Benny said.

"Something about it sounds fishy," agreed Henry.

Kate was bending over the note again. "It doesn't make any more sense than this rhyme," she said. "I mean, why would Thane save Sally's life and then steal from her family?"

Violet had a thought. "Do you think that rhyme holds the truth?"

Kate waved that away. "I doubt it, Violet. This was just a parlor game. I remember my grandmother talking about Thane's rhymes and riddles, and how much fun she had trying to solve them."

But the Aldens weren't convinced it was just a game. They had a feeling there was more to it than that. A lot more.

CHAPTER 5

Spotting a Leopard?

The children worked on the old desk all morning. After a lunch of grilled cheese sandwiches and coleslaw, they took a break to play Frisbee and cool off in the pond. It wasn't long, though, before they were hard at work once more. When Benny stopped to rub his shoulder, Jessie spoke up.

"You'd better rest a while, Benny," she advised, "or you'll be sore in the morning."

The youngest Alden didn't need to be coaxed. In no time at all, he was sprawled out on the floor nearby with a *Wizard of Oz* coloring book and a jar of crayons.

"Boy, this desk has taken a real beating," said Henry, shaking his head.

Violet watched as her older brother ran a finger along a deep scratch in the wood. "I see what you mean, Henry," she said. "I guess it needs a bit of a touch-up. You know, with some paint or stain."

"Well, if you ask me," said Jessie, stepping back to admire their work, "it's looking pretty good."

Violet went over and stood beside her older sister. "Now that you mention it, the walnut does have a nice shine to it," she said. "I can't wait to show Kate."

"I wish we could solve the mystery for her," said Benny.

"So do I," agreed Violet. "I really like Kate."

"Which mystery?" Henry wanted to know. "The mystery of Ethan Cape or the mystery of Thane Pace?"

Jessie laughed. "I guess we got more than we bargained for."

"Two for the price of one," Henry said, half-joking.

Violet pulled a clean rag from the wicker basket. "Maybe we should concentrate on one mystery at a time."

"I was thinking the same thing," said Henry. "How about if we stick with Thane's rhyme?"

Jessie agreed. "At least we'll have something to work with."

Violet wiped away a cobweb from under the desk. "I have a funny feeling there's more to that rhyme than Kate thinks."

"You could be right," said Henry as he rubbed wax into the wood. "It must've been hidden away for a reason."

Benny was deep in thought. "You don't think . . ." he said, and then stopped.

"Are you wondering if Thane really did take that money?" Violet asked in a gentle voice. Then she quickly added, "I've been wondering about that, too, Benny. But I have a strong hunch he didn't."

Benny turned to Jessie. "Do you think Thane was a thief?"

Jessie didn't answer right away. Finally, she said, "No, I don't."

Benny looked up at his older brother. "What do you say, Henry?"

"Thane saved Sally's life," Henry answered, standing up straight. He arched his back and stretched. "I can't believe somebody that brave could be a thief."

"I don't believe it, either," said Benny, looking relieved.

"The important thing right now," put in Jessie, "is to figure out that strange rhyme."

Benny frowned a little. "What did it say again?"

Jessie smiled at her little brother. "Don't worry, Benny," she assured him. "I jotted it down in my notebook. We can check it out again later."

Henry and Violet exchanged smiles. They could always count on Jessie to be organized.

Just then, Benny groaned. "Uh-oh."

"Oh, Benny, is your shoulder still bothering you?" Jessie asked him, a worried look on her face.

Benny shook his head. "My shoulder's okay, but . . . I can't find a green crayon."

"Oh," said Jessie, sounding relieved. "Well, just use another color."

Benny shook his head again. "It's the Emerald City, Jessie, and emeralds are green."

Violet went over to check it out. After digging through the crayons, she said, "You're right, Benny. No green."

"Why don't you call it the Ruby City?" Henry suggested, hiding a smile. "Then you can color it red."

Benny thought about this. "I guess that'll work."

"Or . . ." put in Violet, "you can color it with a yellow crayon and then with a blue crayon."

"Two colors?"

"Watch what happens, Benny." Violet colored one of the towers in the Emerald City with a yellow crayon. Then she colored over it with blue.

Benny's jaw dropped. "It turned green!"

"That's what happens when you mix yellow and blue together, Benny," Violet explained, smiling at her little brother. "The two colors make one brand new color—green!"

"Cool!" Benny was grinning from ear to ear.

Kate poked her head into the room. "Well, just look at that desk!" she said. "It's amazing what can be done in a short time."

"We're almost finished here," Henry told her.

"Well, I see you've added something new," remarked Josh. He had come into the room behind Kate.

Kate couldn't help laughing. "Actually, Josh, I've added something old," she told him. "Come and take a look."

"Well, it sure fits in nicely," Josh said approvingly. Then he turned to his wife, who was trailing behind. "Don't you think so, Vanessa?"

Vanessa nodded a little. Then she picked up a magazine and began to flip through the glossy pages.

"The desk belonged to my great-grandfather," Kate explained. "I checked all the old photos, and this is exactly where it used to be. Right here in this very spot. And see that painting?" She pointed to a framed watercolor of green hills. "That painting always hung on the wall behind the desk."

"It's such a lovely landscape," said Violet, who was very artistic and had an eye for beauty. "I've been admiring it all day."

Kate smiled. "'The Emerald Isle' is my favorite painting in the house."

"The Emerald Isle?" Benny glanced over at the painting curiously. "Is that like the Emerald City in *The Wizard of Oz?*"

Henry shook his head. "The Emerald Isle is another name for Ireland, Benny," he said, putting an arm around his little brother.

"Yes, the artist was from Ireland," put in Kate. "Margaret O'Malley loved painting the green hills of her home."

"Oh, I get it!" Benny snapped his fingers. "Ireland has green hills, and an emerald is green!"

Henry gave him the thumbs-up sign.

"You catch on fast, Benny."

"Margaret O'Malley?" Vanessa tossed her magazine aside. "Never heard of her."

"Oh, she wasn't famous. No, not at all. Painting was just one of her hobbies," Kate was quick to explain. "You see, Margaret O'Malley worked for the family when my grandmother was growing up."

Vanessa was tapping her chin, her eyes fixed on the watercolor. "That's just the right shade of green."

Josh gave his wife a puzzled look. "The right shade?"

"To go with the chairs in our living room," Vanessa told him. Then she turned to Kate. "I can write a check for it now."

The children all looked at one another. They couldn't help thinking that Lindsay was right. Vanessa seemed to want everything she saw.

"Nothing in this house is for sale," Kate told Vanessa firmly. "Nothing at all."

The young woman clicked her tongue, then turned on her heel and stormed out of the room.

Josh apologized for his wife's behavior. "Vanessa can be pushy sometimes. But she has a good heart."

After Josh left, Kate shook her head. "That man has his hands full, I'm afraid," she said, keeping her voice low. Then, changing the subject, she reached into her pocket and pulled out some dollar bills. "Let me give you something for all your hard work."

Jessie spoke up. "Please put your money away, Kate."

"We like helping," added Violet. And Henry and Benny nodded.

Kate hesitated for a moment, then tucked the money away again. "Well, then, let me treat you to a night out. After dinner we can catch a performance of *The Wizard of Oz*. How does that sound?"

It sounded wonderful. It wasn't long before they were following a line of people into the theater. The children sat wide-eyed throughout the play. They could hardly believe they were right there in Kansas—Dorothy's home. And when the actors took their bows, they joined Kate in clapping their hands as hard as they could.

It was late by the time they finally got back to Wiggin Place. After getting ready for bed, the Aldens met for a late-night meeting in the room that Violet and Jessie shared.

"Read it again, Jessie," urged Benny, who was swinging his feet from the edge of the bed.

"Maybe it'll make sense this time," added Violet.

Nodding, Jessie opened her little notebook and read aloud. *"Where leopards get spotted/ a clue will appear./ Just take a look under/ the little dog's ear."*

Nobody said anything for a moment. Then Jessie glanced up from her notebook. "Leopards get spotted at the zoo," she pointed out.

"That's true," said Henry.

"Don't forget about the jungle," Benny reminded them with a big smile. "I bet you can spot plenty of leopards there."

This made Violet think. "Wait a minute,"

she said, looking over at her brothers and sister. "Where have we heard that before?"

Jessie looked puzzled. So did Henry and Benny.

"Oh!" Benny's eyes widened as he suddenly caught Violet's meaning. "That's what Sally called the woods out back."

"Exactly!" Violet nodded.

"Do you really think Thane hid a clue in the woods?" Jessie asked doubtfully.

"It's possible," said Violet.

"Even so," Henry pointed out, "I'm not sure it'd still be there after all these years."

"Maybe not," admitted Violet. "But it's worth checking out."

Jessie and Henry weren't sure about this. Still, it couldn't hurt to take a look around the woods in the morning.

CHAPTER 6

The Jungle

"You know, Kate," Vanessa said at breakfast the next morning, "if it's a check that bothers you, I can arrange to give you cash for your painting."

Josh was frowning at his wife. But she didn't stop.

"And that goes for the necklace, too, of course," she said.

Kate was pouring syrup over her pancakes. "You really must stop this, Vanessa," she said.

The professor suddenly spoke up. "Don't

be too hasty, Kate. None of us is getting any younger, right?" he said with a forced laugh. "We could all use a bit of money tucked away for our old age."

Jessie caught Henry's eye. Why did Professor Brewer care about this?

"Yes, yes, that's worth considering!" Vanessa shot the professor a grateful smile. "A little nest egg, Kate. Isn't that more practical than a cluttered-up house?"

Violet didn't like to hear this. She just had to say something. "Kate's house isn't filled with clutter. It's filled with her family history."

Josh turned to his wife. "Violet's right. That's part of its charm."

Vanessa frowned. "Josh, please!" She looked sharply at her husband. "You're not helping matters."

Kate shook her head firmly. "I won't part with my family's past."

Vanessa looked as if she wanted to argue, but she didn't. She just shrugged a little. "Suit yourself," she said.

Turning to the professor, Kate added,

"Thank you for your concern, Professor Brewer, but I'll manage just fine in my old age."

Jessie glanced at the professor. His mouth was set in a hard, thin line.

"I was thinking of baking this morning, Benny," Lindsay said as she stood up to clear the table. "How does a batch of peanut-butter cookies sound?"

Benny broke into a grin. "Sounds great!"

"Better watch out," Henry said, half-joking. "Cookies have a way of disappearing when Benny's around."

This made Kate smile a little. "Any plans for today, kids?" she asked, pushing her chair back.

"We thought we'd explore the jungle," said Jessie.

"If you don't mind, Kate," Violet was quick to add.

Kate didn't mind at all. "Just watch out for tigers and lions!" she said with a teasing twinkle in her eye.

After helping with the dishes, the Aldens filled a thermos with pink lemonade. Then they filed out the door. "Anything unusual can be a clue," Henry reminded his brother and sisters.

"Thane might've carved something on a rock," added Violet, "or into a tree."

Benny fell into step beside Henry. "And don't forget to keep a sharp eye out for leopards."

Jessie couldn't help laughing. "I doubt we'll come across any leopards in Kansas, Benny."

As they followed the winding path through the woods, the four children checked every rock along the way looking for any strange markings. They inspected hollowed-out trees and looked under bushes. They searched and searched and searched. But by noon they still hadn't found anything that would help solve the mystery.

"I guess we're on the wrong track," Violet had to admit as they sat together on a fallen log.

"Sure looks that way, Violet," agreed Henry.

"I don't get it." Benny held out his pink cup as Jessie poured the lemonade. "This is where Thane's rhyme was leading us. I'm sure of it."

"Maybe the clue disappeared a long time ago," suggested Jessie, pulling a twig from her hair. "Just like Henry said."

The four Aldens were deep in thought when a familiar voice caught their attention. They didn't mean to eavesdrop. But from where they were sitting, the children couldn't help overhearing.

"I'm telling you, it's not as easy as that . . . No, no . . . this place is always filled to the rafters."

"Isn't that Lindsay?" Benny asked.

Violet nodded. "I wonder why she sounds so upset."

"Look, I just don't think I can pull it off." Lindsay was talking loudly now. "I told you, I'll do my best to get it to you. That's right . . . old and blue."

"Did you hear that?" Jessie whispered.

Henry nodded. None of them liked the sound of this.

Just then, Lindsay stepped into the clearing. When she spotted the Aldens, she quickly pocketed her cell phone. "Oh, hi, kids!" she said. "I, um . . . was just out for a breath of fresh air." She bit her lip nervously. "Guess I'd better . . . get back to work." Before the children could say a word, she hurried away.

"That was a bit strange, don't you think?" remarked Jessie.

"She said she didn't think she could pull it off," put in Benny. "I wonder what she meant by that."

Henry shrugged. "There's no way of knowing."

"Do you think she's up to something?" Benny wanted to know.

"I hope not." Violet didn't like to suspect Lindsay of doing anything wrong. Still, it did sound suspicious.

The four children fell silent for a while. Then Benny spoke up.

"I vote we take another look through the woods after lunch," he said, still thinking about Thane's rhyme.

Henry nodded. "I guess it's possible we overlooked some kind of clue."

"Let's not say anything to Kate," suggested Violet. "We don't want to get her hopes up for nothing."

"Good idea, Violet," Jessie said, as they headed to the house for lunch. "We'll try to figure things out first."

They refused to give up. After toasted tomato sandwiches, fruit salad, and peanut-butter cookies, they went back to the woods. They looked for anything unusual as they made their way along every path. Once, twice, three times. But it was no use. By the end of the afternoon, they were still no closer to solving the mystery.

"Did you enjoy your safari through the jungle?" Kate wanted to know, as they relaxed in the front room after dinner.

"We didn't have any luck," Benny told her. "We tried to spot a leopard like the rhyme said, but—"

Henry poked him, then Benny remembered they weren't supposed to talk about the mystery.

Kate's eyebrows shot up. "Oh, are you trying to figure out Thane's rhyme?"

The children looked at one another. They didn't want to lie, but they also knew it was best not to get Kate's hopes up yet.

Henry quickly changed the subject. "Is that your family album, Kate?"

"Why, yes, Henry!" Kate reached for her family album from the coffee table. "Would you care to take a look?" As the children nodded eagerly, she turned to the professor sitting nearby. "How about you, Professor Brewer? Will you join us?"

The professor slowly lowered his newspaper. "I'm busy at the moment."

"Maybe later, then," Kate said with a little smile.

As Kate turned the pages of the album, Jessie couldn't help noticing that the professor was staring at the photograph above the fireplace. Now and again, his lips would curl up into a smile. It seemed rather odd to Jessie.

"Here's one of Sally. It was taken in 1904, just a few days after she fell through the ice." Kate was tapping a finger under a faded old photograph.

Henry, Jessie, Violet, and Benny gathered round. A young girl, about Benny's age, was sitting at a table shaped like a half moon. The girl had delicate features, and long dark hair that hung round her shoulders. She was holding a book in front of her.

"Why isn't she smiling?" Benny wanted to know.

Violet had an answer. "Nobody smiled in those old photographs, Benny. You see, it wasn't easy getting your picture taken in the olden days. People had to hold the same pose for almost half an hour."

Henry, who kept looking from the photo to a corner of the room and back again, said, "Isn't that the same table?"

They all followed his gaze to a table in a shadowy corner. Beside it was a straight-backed chair with padded arms.

"What sharp eyes, Henry!" exclaimed Kate. "Yes, that's the very spot where the photograph was taken. That half-moon table has always been in that corner, close to the oval window with the frosted glass. I've been trying to find the same wallpaper they had back then," she added, pointing to the photograph again. "See the big roses all over it?"

Just then, the professor's shoes squeaked, making them look up. As he left the room, Kate lowered her voice. "I'm looking foward to a peaceful day tomorrow. The professor's going away on some kind of outing." She let out a sigh. "Even Josh and Vanessa will be gone before breakfast."

"Where's everybody going?" Benny wanted to know.

Jessie gave her little brother a warning look. "That's not really any of our business, Benny."

Kate laughed a little. "I imagine they're going sightseeing, Benny." She stood up and yawned. "Well, it's been a long day. Time to hit the sack." With that, she said good-night and went upstairs.

"It's been a long day for us, too," Henry reminded them. "Why don't we call it a night?"

As they started for the door, Violet noticed that Jessie was still bent over the photograph album. "What is it, Jessie?"

"It's the strangest thing . . ." Jessie lifted her head. "I think Sally's reading a book about leopards. In the photo, I mean."

"Leopards . . . ?" repeated Henry, his eyes wide with surprise.

Violet sat down beside her older sister. "Are you sure, Jessie?"

"I can't be certain," said Jessie. "It's hard to make out the title."

The youngest Alden raced out of the room. When he returned, he was holding a magnifying glass. "I told you we'd need it," he said, handing it to Jessie.

"What would we do without you, Benny?" Henry said with a smile.

After studying the photograph through the magnifying glass, Jessie said, "Guess what? The title of Sally's book is *How the Leopard Got Its Spots*."

"Wow!" cried Violet, a look of astonishment on her face.

Henry said, "I've read that story in

school. Rudyard Kipling wrote it."

"What's it about, Henry?" Benny wanted to know.

Henry perched on the arm of a chair. "Well, at the beginning of the story, the leopard's just a plain color—kind of brownish yellow. When he goes hunting in the desert, the other animals can't see him."

Benny was curious. "Why can't they see him?"

"Because he blends in with the desert," explained Henry. "But then the other animals decide to live in the jungle. Of course, then the leopard's got a real problem. He doesn't blend in with the background and the other animals can see him coming. So the leopard goes to his friend for help, and the man dips his fingers into black ink and—"

"Gives the leopard spots!" finished Benny.

"You guessed it." Henry smiled at his little brother. "After that, the leopard blends in with the jungle background, and becomes a great hunter again."

"Is that a true story?" Benny asked,

after a moment's thought.

Jessie shook her head firmly. "Rudyard Kipling made it up, Benny."

"So, do you think the rhyme's leading us to Sally's book?" Violet wondered.

"Got to be." Henry sounded very sure.

"That means we have to find it," Jessie realized. "Sally's book, I mean."

"Come on!" Benny was already halfway to the door. "Let's try the reading room first."

The others knew there was no stopping Benny. "We're right behind you, Sherlock," said Henry as they followed their little brother along the hallway.

Inside the reading room, Jessie flipped on a light switch and glanced around at all the shelves crowded with books. Even the tables were piled high. "It won't take as long if we split up," she suggested in her practical way.

Henry and Benny set to work checking out the books stacked on the tables. Jessie and Violet searched the shelves, looking for anything by Rudyard Kipling.

After some time had passed, Jessie walked over to her sister and said, "I haven't had any luck, have you, Violet?"

Just then Violet's jaw dropped. "Here it is!" she whispered. It was all she could do to keep from shouting.

Henry and Benny rushed over. "Did you find it?" said Henry.

Violet pulled a faded orange-colored book down from the shelf and opened it. "Oh, there's an inscription!" she exclaimed. Then she read it aloud. "To our Sally, from Mother and Father."

Benny rubbed his hands together. "Now we're getting somewhere!"

It was late, but the Aldens were determined to search for the hidden clue. As they stood together in a circle of yellow light from the table lamp, Jessie began to turn the pages slowly . . . slowly . . . slowly.

"I bet there's a note stuck inside the book," said Benny, sounding excited.

Henry added, "Or maybe a message scribbled on a page."

They checked out every word and every illustration. But they didn't find any note stuck inside or any scribbled messages. Their only small discovery was a page with the corner turned down.

"I guess Sally wanted to mark her spot," suggested Violet.

But Jessie wasn't so sure. "Unless . . ." A sudden thought came to her.

"Unless what, Jessie?" Benny wanted to know.

"Unless Thane marked the spot."

The others looked at Jessie in surprise. "You think there's a clue hidden on this page?" Violet asked.

"But it's just an illustration," Benny pointed out.

"That's true, Benny," said Jessie. "But remember how the rhyme goes?" She recited the last few lines. *"Just take a look under/ The little dog's ear.* Maybe there's a dog in the illustration."

The Aldens examined the glossy page carefully. They found zebras and giraffes, lions and tigers, elephants and hippos, monkeys and leopards. But no dogs.

"What now?" Benny wanted to know, his shoulders slumped with disappointment.

None of them had an answer to that question.

CHAPTER 7

The Little Dog's Ear

The Aldens got up early the next morning. They wanted to surprise Kate with a special breakfast. While they worked, they talked about Thane's rhyme.

"Maybe it really was just a parlor game," Jessie was saying as she sliced a cantalope into wedges.

Henry, who was keeping an eye on the sizzling sausages, looked over. "Or maybe Thane left Wiggin Place before he had a chance to hide any clues."

"Anything's possible," admitted Violet,

scrambling eggs in a large bowl. "Still, it wouldn't hurt to take another look at Sally's book."

"It's worth a shot," declared Benny. He didn't like to give up. As he placed a dish of strawberry jam on the table, he added, "We *will* solve the mystery, won't we?"

"Sure we will," said Henry. Then he added honestly, "At least, we'll do our best."

"Well, what's all this?" Kate asked, her eyes wide as she walked into the kitchen. Lindsay was close behind.

"We made breakfast," Jessie said with a smile. "You're just in time."

"Everything smells wonderful!" said Kate, pulling up a chair.

"It sure does." Lindsay slipped into the empty seat beside Kate. "I feel like one of the guests."

Over breakfast, the children noticed that Kate seemed unusually quiet. Violet couldn't help asking if anything was wrong.

Kate smiled, but it wasn't much of a smile. "Nothing for you to worry about,

Violet. Everything will work out."

The Aldens looked at one another with concern. Why wasn't Kate her usual cheery self?

"If there's a problem, maybe we can help," offered Henry. He passed the platter of sausages to Benny.

Kate let out a sigh. "Well, this is going to sound a little odd, but—"

"The bluebird necklace has disappeared," Lindsay blurted out.

"What . . . ?" Benny almost choked on his toast.

Jessie stared over at Kate in surprise. "You can't mean . . . the necklace that belonged to your grandmother?"

Nodding, Kate said, "I left it out on my dresser. At least, that's where I thought I'd left it. You see, the clasp was a bit loose, and I was going to take it into town to have it fixed." A frown crossed her kind face. "It's the strangest thing. When I got up this morning, it was gone," she went on. "The necklace has vanished."

"I can't believe it!" said Violet.

Henry was baffled. "But it couldn't just . . . vanish."

"Apparently it did, Henry," put in Lindsay.

"I don't understand it," said Jessie. "What could've happened?"

Benny spoke up. "I know what happened."

All eyes turned to the youngest Alden. "What, Benny?" Kate asked.

"Somebody stole it!"

Kate held up a hand. "Now, now, Benny," she cautioned him. "No need to think that. I refuse to believe anyone in this house would steal my grandmother's necklace. I've simply misplaced it, that's all. We mustn't jump to any conclusions."

Jessie agreed. "I guess we shouldn't suspect people until we're certain it was actually stolen."

Lindsay reached out and placed a hand gently on Kate's arm. "After I run a few errands in town, I'll help you look for it. We'll turn this place inside out if we have to!"

"We'll help, too," Jessie volunteered, and the others nodded.

Kate brushed some crumbs from the front of her dress. "I appreciate the offers," she told them. "But I'll give my bedroom a thorough going-over. I'm sure that'll do the trick. The necklace must be in my room somewhere."

After breakfast, the children discussed the strange disappearance while they cleaned the kitchen. "That necklace means so much to Kate," said Violet, handing Jessie the sausage platter to wash. "I sure hope she finds it."

"She won't," said Benny.

Jessie looked at her little brother. "Why do you say that, Benny?"

"Because Vanessa stole it."

"Benny!" Jessie exclaimed. "You shouldn't say things like that."

"But I'm pretty sure she did, Jessie," Benny said, carefully drying his cracked pink cup. "Vanessa wants everything she sees, remember? Even that painting of the Emerald Isle."

Violet carried the empty glasses over to the sink. "I know Vanessa seems a bit spoiled, Benny," she said, "but that doesn't make her a thief."

"It is weird, though, about the necklace suddenly disappearing," said Henry.

Jessie turned to face her older brother. "Even if it was stolen, Henry, Vanessa isn't the only suspect."

Henry looked at her, puzzled. So did Violet and Benny.

"I think we should include the professor on our list."

Violet gave her sister a questioning glance. "The professor?"

Nodding, Jessie told them how she'd caught the professor staring up at the photograph above the fireplace. "He had the strangest smile on his face—as if he knew something no one else did." She paused for a moment. "Vanessa might not be the only one interested in the bluebird necklace."

The others thought about this for a moment. Sally was wearing the necklace in that photograph over the fireplace. Was it the family heirloom that held the professor's attention? Nobody knew. But they had to admit it was possible. Hadn't the professor tried to convince Kate to sell her family heirloom? Didn't he say she'd be better off with a little money tucked away for her old age?

"There's somebody else we should consider," Henry told them.

"Who's that?" Benny wanted to know.

"Lindsay," Henry said.

"Oh, Henry!" cried Jessie. "I don't think Lindsay has the heart to be a thief."

"We have to consider everybody," insisted Henry. "And remember what she said on the phone?"

Jessie nodded. "She said, 'I just don't think I can pull it off.'"

"And that's not all," Benny recalled. "She was talking about something old and blue." He looked around at the others. "Kate's necklace is old and blue!"

"That does sound suspicious," admitted Jessie.

"But why would she want to hurt Kate

like that, Henry?" Violet couldn't believe Lindsay would do something so awful.

"I'm not sure, Violet," Henry said. "But maybe we should keep an eye on all of them for a while—Vanessa, Lindsay, and the professor."

After finishing the dishes, the Aldens headed for the reading room. Sitting cross-legged on the rug, they searched carefully through Sally's book for clues. But once again they were disappointed.

Benny drew his eyebrows together in a frown. "It doesn't make sense," he said. "The clue should be here."

"But . . . where?" asked Violet.

Henry shrugged. "That's a good question."

Just then, Kate walked into the room. "Oh, I didn't know you were in here," she said, looking surprised when she saw the Aldens. "I'm trying to tidy up a bit while I'm searching," she told them, glancing down at her armful of old novels. "My night table was buried under books."

"You sure have a lot," Benny remarked,

as Kate added to the stack of books on the coffee table. "Almost as many as the Greenfield Public Library."

Kate laughed at this. "Well, most of my books are old and dog-eared, Benny. But I still treasure them."

As Kate turned to go, Violet said, "No luck yet?"

Kate shook her head. "No, but it'll turn up by the end of the day," she said, trying to sound upbeat. "Just wait and see, Violet." Then she closed the door behind her.

The Aldens soon turned their attention back to Sally's book. They were more determined than ever to solve the mystery for Kate.

"There must be something we're not seeing," Jessie said. "Don't you think, Henry?"

Henry didn't answer. As he looked down at Sally's book, an idea began to form in his mind. Then he suddenly slapped his forehead with the palm of his hand. "Of course!" he exclaimed, laughing a little.

"Don't keep us in the dark, Henry," Benny said. "What's up?"

"Remember what Kate said about her books?" Henry sounded excited.

The others stared at their older brother. They looked totally confused.

Seeing their puzzled faces, Henry explained, "She said they were old and—"

Jessie's eyes widened as she caught Henry's drift. She finished her brother's sentence for him. "Dog-eared!"

"Oh, I can't believe we didn't think of that!" Violet clapped her hands.

"Dog-eared?" Benny repeated, not understanding.

"They say a book's dog-eared, Benny," Jessie was quick to explain, "when some of the pages have been turned down at the corners. You know, from people marking their spot."

"Oh, I get it!" Benny said in sudden understanding. "The turned-down part looks like a dog's ear, right?"

"Right," said Henry.

"No wonder we weren't getting anywhere," Jessie realized, flipping to the end of the book. "Thane must've hidden the clue under a corner of the page."

They all held their breath, as Jessie lifted the flap. Sure enough, a message had been scribbled under the little dog's ear.

The Aldens let out a cheer. Figuring out clues was always fun.

"What does it say, Jessie?" Benny gave his sister a nudge.

With a puzzled frown, Jessie read the message out loud:

> *Blue and yellow,*
> *yellow and blue,*
> *two make one,*
> *a gem of a clue!*

"What do you think it means?" wondered Violet.

Jessie shrugged. So did Henry.

"It's a mystery," Benny said with a grin. "I love mysteries!"

CHAPTER 8

Two Make One

"It's not much to go on," Jessie remarked as she made a copy of the rhyme.

Benny was scratching his head. "What I don't understand," he said, "is how two can make one."

Henry shrugged. "Beats me."

"I can't understand it, either," admitted Violet. "Thane's clues are tough to figure out."

The children puzzled over the strange rhyme all morning. They thought and thought, but they couldn't come up with any answers. Everyone was stumped.

"I have an idea," Violet said when she caught a whiff of flowers coming through the opened window. "Let's pack a picnic lunch and go for a bike ride."

The others were quick to agree. "We could use a break," said Henry.

After telling Kate about their plans, the Aldens loaded sandwiches, apples, and a large thermos of lemonade into Henry's backpack, then set off on the bikes Kate kept for her guests. Putting all thoughts of the mystery aside for a while, they pedaled happily through the countryside.

By the time they returned to Wiggin Place, the afternoon sun was getting hot, the rhyme was still a big question mark, and the necklace was still missing.

"Kate's been tearing her room apart all day," Violet remarked. "I think she's beginning to give up hope." The children were sitting at the umbrella table on the stone patio, sipping ice-cold cranberry juice from tall glasses.

Jessie tugged her notebook from her back

pocket. "One mystery at a time, remember?"

Henry agreed. "Let's take another look at that rhyme."

Nodding, Jessie read it aloud. *"Blue and yellow/ yellow and blue/ two make one/ a gem of a clue!"*

"What about Kate's necklace?" said Violet, after a moment's thought. "Isn't it blue and yellow?"

Jessie was quick to agree. "A bluebird charm on a yellow-gold chain."

"And the blue and yellow make one necklace," added Violet, pouring Benny another glass of cranberry juice.

Henry was nodding his head. "You might be on to something, Violet."

Jessie said, "The clues seem to fit."

"But Kate's necklace doesn't have any gems on it," argued Benny. "Not even a single diamond. Blue and yellow are supposed to make one gem of a clue. Remember?"

"Good point, Benny," Henry said, arms folded, leaning back in his chair.

"But . . . what else could it mean?" Jessie

was bending over her notebook again.

"It's a mystery," Violet said, laughing a little. "As Grandfather would say, Wiggin Place has more mysteries than you can shake a stick at."

"And the mysteries aren't easy to solve," added Henry.

"Sally Crawford is the key," said Benny.

The others had to admit their little brother was right. All the mysteries had something to do with Sally.

Jessie started adding everything up on her fingers. "There's the mystery of Ethan Cape. Didn't the famous photographer come all the way to Kansas just to take Sally's picture? And how about the missing necklace? It once belonged to Sally."

"And don't forget about Thane Pace," put in Violet. "He saved Sally's life."

Henry added, "Even the rhymes were meant for her."

"I wish we knew more about Sally's secret," Jessie said, lost in thought. "The one she wanted to share after Ethan Cape's visit."

"Speaking of Ethan Cape," said Violet, reaching for a book on the empty chair beside her, "looks like somebody's reading his biography."

"Probably Kate," guessed Henry.

"I'm sure you're right, Henry." Violet began to thumb through the pages. "Wow, there's all sorts of photographs in here." Her eyes were shining. "Ethan was a genius with the camera."

"Sounds like a good book," Jessie remarked. "Maybe you can borrow it when Kate's finished."

But Violet was only half-listening. She had come to something that made her stop and stare. "This is strange," she said in a puzzled voice. "Here's a photo taken in the olden days."

Benny, Jessie, and Henry crowded around to take a look. A middle-aged woman in a high-necked blouse and long skirt was sitting at a table shaped like a half moon. She was wearing a white apron and matching cap.

"That lady must have been a cook,"

observed Benny. "At least, that's how she's dressed."

Henry nodded his head. "That's what I was just thinking."

Jessie looked at her sister. "What's strange about that, Violet?"

"Well, maybe this is just a weird coincidence," said Violet, "but isn't there something about this photograph that looks familiar?"

Jessie took a closer look. "Now that you mention it," she said, "it reminds me of Sally's photograph. The one taken when she was Benny's age."

Peering over Violet's shoulder, Henry nodded. "There's a half-moon table in both pictures."

"But that's not all," put in Violet. "Did you notice the background?"

Jessie looked. "Oh, my goodness!" she cried. "An oval window with frosted glass!"

"And wallpaper with big roses all over it," added Benny.

Jessie nodded. "That can mean only one thing."

Benny looked at her. "What?"

"The cook's photograph was taken right here at Wiggin Place."

Henry shook his head. "This is getting weirder and weirder."

"What does it say under the picture, Violet?" Jessie asked.

As Violet scanned the small print, her eyes widened.

"What is it?" Henry asked.

Before Violet could answer, the professor stepped out onto the patio. When he caught sight of the book Violet was holding, he rushed over and snatched it away. "How dare you!" He sounded upset. "You have no business touching my grandfather's book! It's a good thing I came back early."

Violet's eyes widened in alarm. "But I thought—"

The professor walked away before Violet could finish. Then he suddenly wheeled around to face them again. "This must never happen again," he said in an icy voice. "I'm warning you, you'll regret it if it does!" And then he was gone.

The Aldens looked at one another in disbelief.

"It was just a mistake," Violet said in a small voice. "I didn't know the book belonged to the professor's grandfather."

Jessie patted her sister gently on the shoulder. "You didn't do anything wrong, Violet," said Jessie, trying to comfort her. "The professor wouldn't even give you a chance to explain."

"Wait a minute," said Henry. "Didn't the professor say he wasn't interested in Ethan Cape?"

Jessie nodded slowly. "Why would he pretend he wasn't?"

"That's just what I was wondering," said Henry.

CHAPTER 9

Scrabble, Anyone?

No sooner had the professor gone inside, than Lindsay stepped out the door. "I thought I'd find you here," she told the Aldens with a smile. "I just wanted to let you know I'll be leaving in the morning."

The children were surprised to hear this. "You mean you won't be working here anymore?" Benny wondered.

"Oh, I'll be back, Benny," Lindsay assured the youngest Alden. "I'm just going to take a few days off to attend my cousin's wedding." She sat down in the empty chair beside Violet. "I really wasn't planning to go at all, you know. I told my cousin if I could do it in one day, that'd be different. But it's too long a drive for that. I just couldn't pull it off. And how could I leave Kate with a houseful of guests any longer than that?"

Jessie and Henry exchanged glances. That must have been the phone conversation they'd overheard in the woods!

"I was determined to keep the whole wedding thing to myself," Lindsay went on. "Only, Kate found the invitation in my apron pocket and put her foot down. There's no way she'll let me miss a family wedding."

Violet nodded in sudden understanding. That's what Lindsay had shoved into her pocket when they'd startled her that first day—the wedding invitation!

Benny stared at Lindsay. "You were talking on the phone about something old and blue."

"Oh, you heard that, did you?" Lindsay

was smiling. "It's a tradition for brides, Benny. 'Something old, something new...'"

"'Something borrowed, something blue!'" finished Violet, in a singsong voice.

"Exactly!" Lindsay laughed. "My cousin has her heart set on borrowing a lace hanky that's been in my family for years. It has tiny blue flowers on it."

"Something old and blue," said Jessie, catching Henry's eye. He nodded. They could cross Lindsay off their list of suspects.

Lindsay pushed her chair back. "Well, I'd better check on dinner. I've got a roast chicken in the oven."

"We'll help," Jessie offered, speaking for them all. "We can set the dining room table."

"It sure is funny about that photograph," Henry said as he set plates around the table.

"Are you talking about the lady in the white cap?" asked Benny.

Henry nodded. "I wonder who she was."

Violet had an answer. "Margaret O'Malley. At least, that's what it said under the picture."

"Margaret O'Malley?" repeated Jessie, as she smoothed out the tablecloth. The name sounded familiar, but she couldn't quite put her finger on where she'd heard it.

Violet went to shut the opened door. "The painting of the Emerald Isle, remember?" she reminded them in a hushed voice. "Margaret O'Malley was the artist."

Henry's eyebrows shot up. "Oh, that's right!"

"She must have been the family cook," said Jessie, every bit as surprised as her older brother.

Benny nodded. "Kate said she worked here when Sally was growing up!"

"That's not all." Violet set a vase of daisies in the middle of the table. "Margaret O'Malley's photograph was taken in 1904."

"Are you sure?" Henry looked uncertain.

Violet nodded. "Quite sure, Henry."

"But . . . that's the same year Sally's photograph was taken," Jessie realized, her eyes huge.

"Sitting at a half-moon table," added Henry, "when she was a little girl."

"There's no doubt about it," Violet concluded. "Those photographs were taken at the same time—right here at Wiggin Place." She nodded her head slowly as it began to sink in. "And I bet they were taken by the same person!"

The Aldens looked at one another. Had Ethan Cape stayed at Wiggin Place more than once?

"According to Kate," Henry said after a moment's thought, "Sally never met Ethan Cape until she was much older—a grandmother."

"All the same, I'm pretty sure Ethan was here before that," Violet insisted, "when Sally was a little girl."

Benny placed the napkins around the table. "Do you think Ethan met Thane Pace back then?"

"I guess it's possible," Henry had to admit. "They were both here around the same time."

"Can you believe it?" Violet couldn't help laughing. "The mysteries are starting to connect!"

"Seems that way," agreed Jessie.

Henry had a suggestion. "Let's keep a lid on this for now. At least until we can make some sense of it."

After dinner, the Aldens challenged Kate to a game of Scrabble. They were hoping it would take her mind off the missing necklace for a while, but it was no use. Before long, Kate called it a night, leaving the four children to finish the game on their own.

While Benny was having a turn, Jessie spoke up. "Kate tries to be cheery, but . . ."

"She's afraid she's seen the last of her necklace," finished Violet, who had pulled her chair closer to her little brother's. She knew he might need help with the harder words.

Henry noticed Benny eyeing the popcorn. "Find any words yet, Sherlock?" he asked, passing the bowl of popcorn across the kitchen table to him.

Benny shifted the letters around on the wooden tile-holder. "Well, it looks like I can spell APE."

"Way to go, Benny!" praised Violet. "And guess what? If you add the letter C, you can turn APE into CAPE."

Benny broke into a smile. "Cool!"

"You can even switch the letters around and turn CAPE into PACE," Jessie pointed out.

"I think I'll stick with CAPE." Benny shoved a handful of popcorn into his mouth, then carefully placed his letters on the board.

As Henry added up Benny's score, Jessie said, "It's funny, isn't it?"

"What's funny about CAPE, Jessie?" Benny asked, raising his eyes.

"It's just . . . the last names are so similar."

Benny looked puzzled. So did Henry and Violet.

"Ethan Cape and Thane Pace, I mean," Jessie explained. "Their last names have exactly the same letters, only switched around."

"You're right, Jessie. I never noticed that before." Henry shrugged a little. "Just a co-incidence, I guess."

But Jessie wasn't so sure. On a hunch, she began fishing around in the bag of lettered tiles. While the others watched, she spelled out the name ETHAN on the scrabble board.

Benny had something to say about this. "You're not supposed to use a person's name, Jessie. It's against the rules."

"I don't think this is part of the game, Benny," said Violet, a finger to her lips.

Jessie switched one letter around, and ETHAN suddenly turned into THANE.

"Wow!" cried Henry, clearly startled.

"I . . . I can't believe it . . . ." Violet pressed her hands to her cheeks. "Their last names have exactly the same letters in them, too!"

"That's got to be more than a coincidence," said Benny, his voice rising with excitement.

"A lot more!" put in Henry, who couldn't get over it.

Jessie giggled. "One thing's for sure," she said. "Ethan Cape never met Thane Pace because—"

"Ethan Cape was Thane Pace!" finished Benny.

The Aldens looked at one another, stunned by their latest discovery.

"That was good detective work, Jessie," praised Henry.

Benny suddenly looked up. "I helped, too."

Jessie smiled over at her little brother. "You sure did. You helped make the word CAPE."

"There's something I don't understand," said Violet. "Why would Thane Pace change his name to Ethan Cape?"

"I have a hunch we won't know the answer to that," Jessie said, "until we figure out the second rhyme."

The Aldens had a feeling they were very close to uncovering the truth.

* * * *

Late in the night, Violet awoke from a strange dream about following the Yellow Brick Road. In her dream, when she got to the Emerald City, she found it was ruby-red! She wanted to paint it green, but there wasn't a drop of green paint in the land. The wizard said he had an answer to the problem. He told Violet, "Two make one."

Violet was still thinking about her dream as she lay awake in the dark. She couldn't help wondering what it meant. And then it suddenly hit her.

"Wake up, Jessie!" she whispered, sitting up.

Jessie began to stir. "What . . . ?"

"I know the answer to the rhyme!" Violet said as she slipped out of bed.

"What are you talking about, Violet?" Jessie asked in a drowsy voice.

"*Two make one/ a gem of a clue!*" Violet recited. "Two colors make one, Jessie. Blue and yellow make green."

Jessie opened her eyes. "And an emerald is green!"

Violet nodded. "Are you thinking what I'm thinking?"

"I think so," said Jessie, throwing her covers back. "Let's go check it out."

After waking Benny and Henry, the Aldens tiptoed downstairs. As they stepped into the front room, Violet stopped so suddenly that Henry almost bumped into her. Somebody was prowling around in the dark with a flashlight!

CHAPTER 10

A Long-Lost Letter

Just as Henry reached for the light switch, there was a terrible crash. The Aldens could hardly believe their eyes when they saw Vanessa standing over a broken lamp, a flashlight in her hand.

"Now you've done it!" she snapped, as doors opened upstairs. "I almost jumped right out of my skin."

There was a sudden rush of footsteps on the stairs. Then Kate appeared in the doorway, struggling to put an arm into her robe. Lindsay was close behind, followed by Josh and the professor. All eyes turned to the lamp on the floor.

"Yes, I broke that," Vanessa told them. "Thanks to the Aldens snooping around down here. They scared me half to death."

"We weren't snooping!" Benny said indignantly. "We were just . . . just . . ." His voice trailed away. He didn't know what to say.

Henry squared his shoulders. "You're the one with the flashlight, Vanessa," he pointed out, looking her right in the eye.

Josh spoke up. "Yeah, what's with that, Vanessa? What are you doing down here with a flashlight?"

Vanessa looked embarrassed, and then angry. "I'm in no mood for this right now," she told her husband. "We'll discuss it in the morning."

Benny thought he knew the answer. "You were trying to steal Kate's painting, weren't you? The one of the Emerald Isle."

"What . . . ?" Vanessa stared at Benny in disbelief. "You think I'm a thief?"

"Well, you stole Kate's necklace, didn't

you?" Benny said accusingly, his hands on his hips.

Kate looked horrified. "Benny, what a terrible thing to say."

Vanessa opened her mouth to speak, then closed it again. Finally, she went over to the window and stared out into the night, looking defeated. After what seemed like forever, she finally spoke. "I am responsible for the missing necklace," she confessed. "But I didn't steal it."

Kate looked over at her, stunned. "Please turn around, Vanessa," she said in a strained voice. "I'd rather not talk to your back."

Vanessa turned around. "I was walking by your room, Kate, and I noticed the necklace on your dresser. I just wanted to try it on, that's all. Before I had a chance to take it off, Lindsay called me downstairs to the phone." Vanessa's voice wavered. There was a long silence while she tried to compose herself. "The next thing I knew, the necklace was gone. I looked everywhere for it, but . . ."

"The clasp was loose," Kate told her.

"I imagine it slipped off."

Josh, who was crouched down by the broken lamp, looked over at his wife. "Why on earth didn't you say something, Vanessa?" He sounded more disappointed than angry.

"I was ashamed," she answered, looking close to tears. "I thought I could find the necklace if I just looked around."

Jessie nodded. "That's why you were using a flashlight. You didn't want anyone to notice the light on."

Vanessa didn't deny it. "The last thing I expected was to run into the Aldens in the middle of the night," she said, sinking into a chair.

Josh was busy trying to fit the pieces of the lamp together. "Looks like a clean break," he said, moving everything off to the side. "A bit of glue should do the trick. If not, we'll buy you a new lamp, Kate."

"I'm not worried about the lamp, Josh," Kate assured him. "I can replace it easily."

"But that's not true of the necklace, is it?" Vanessa buried her head in her hands.

"I'm so sorry, Kate."

"If you mean that, Vanessa," replied Kate, "you'll learn a lesson from this, and respect what belongs to others."

Vanessa nodded, looking truly regretful.

Violet spoke up. "I'm sure we'll find the necklace if everybody looks around for it tomorrow."

Henry nodded. "The secret is teamwork."

Josh perched on the arm of the chair beside his wife. "Henry's right," he told her. "Maybe it's time you and I started acting like a team, Vanessa."

"I'd like that, Josh." Vanessa looked up and smiled a little for the first time.

Kate turned her attention to the Aldens. "And what on earth were the four of you doing down here?"

"Tracking clues," Benny told her proudly.

Henry nodded. "We're getting closer to figuring out Ethan's rhyme, Kate."

Kate looked puzzled, but only for an instant. "Oh, you must be talking about the rhyme you found in the old desk." She sat down on the sofa beside Lindsay. "That was Thane's rhyme, Henry," she corrected. "Remember?"

This made Henry laugh. "Two make one."

Kate looked even more confused.

"They were the same person, Kate," Jessie explained. "Thane changed his name to Ethan Cape."

"At least, that's what we think," added Violet.

"What . . . ?" Kate stared at the children in disbelief.

"Just what kind of game are you kids playing?" The professor, who had been standing in the doorway, suddenly stepped into the room. He didn't look happy.

"It's not a game," Violet said quietly. "We're pretty sure Margaret O'Malley's painting holds a secret." She pointed to the watercolor of the Emerald Isle.

"A secret?" Lindsay's eyes were big. "What kind of secret?"

Henry answered, "Maybe the truth about the past."

Kate smoothed her robe over her knees. "Well, now, this is getting exciting!" she said. "Let's find out what's there," she added. "Would you like to do the honors, Henry?"

Nodding, Henry lifted the painting down from the wall. Everyone gathered round while he gently removed the backing. Sure enough, a folded letter, yellowed with age, had been hidden underneath.

Kate unfolded the letter Henry handed her and read it aloud.

Dear Sally,

I don't know if you'll ever find this letter, but I can't go without leaving the truth behind. As you know, I came out west with my sister on the Orphan Train. I was adopted by one family, and my sister by another. But I never forgot about her. Not for a moment. And so, a few weeks ago, I set out to find her. Imagine my surprise when the young girl I pulled from the icy water turned out to be my long lost sister!

Yes, it's true, Sally. I held you in my arms when we came out together on the Orphan Train. Wrapped up in one of your baby blankets was the bluebird necklace that had belonged to our mother. When I saw it around your neck, I knew the truth. I went to your adopted parents and told them of my discovery. But they refuse to tell you the truth. I think they're afraid of losing you. So they've accused me of theft, and threatened to have me arrested. I have no choice but to leave. (I'll change my name in case they send the law after me. How does Ethan Cape sound?)

But I go with an easy mind, knowing you are in safe hands. In spite of their unfairness to me, I am grateful they've taken such good care of you. I've left you one last riddle to solve—a riddle that will lead to this note. I can only hope your father will give my riddle to you.

I aim to become a great photographer, Sally. Keep the photograph I took of you in your family album. After I make my mark in the world, I'll come back to see you. If you haven't discovered the truth by then, I will tell you everything. Until that time, I shall keep our past a secret.

Your brother,
Thane Pace

For a moment, everyone was too surprised to speak. Finally, Kate broke the silence.

"Amazing," she said, shaking her head in disbelief. "Ethan Cape rode the Orphan Train with my grandmother!"

"He was your great-uncle, Kate," Josh was quick to point out.

"Why, yes. I . . . I suppose so." Kate stared wide-eyed as the truth began to sink in.

The professor dropped into a chair. "That fills in the missing gap in those early years of Ethan's life."

This made Kate turn in surprise. "What's your interest in this, professor?"

The professor hesitated, then he said, "I'm not the person you think I am, Kate."

Kate blinked in disbelief. "You tricked me?"

"I did."

"But . . . why?" said Kate. "Why would you do such a thing?"

"I should never have deceived you, Kate," the professor said. "But I was afraid you wouldn't let me stay if you knew the truth." He looked over at the picture above the fireplace. "You see, I'm a collector of Ethan Cape's works."

Kate's mouth had dropped open. "Of course!" she cried. "I thought your voice sounded familiar—you're the man I spoke with on the phone a few months ago. You wanted to buy the photograph of my grandmother."

"That's right."

"You wouldn't take no for an answer," Kate went on. "As I recall, I was forced to hang up on you."

The professor managed a weak smile. "I know I was a bit too pushy," he admitted. "That's why I thought it best to pretend to be someone else—a professor just here on vacation."

Kate frowned. "You figured you could convince me to sell my grandmother's photograph," she concluded. "That explains why you kept talking about putting money away for my old age. How could you do something like that?"

The professor looked down at his hands. "Because family history means a great deal to me, too, Kate."

Jessie's jaw suddenly dropped. "Oh, my goodness!"

The others turned to look at her. "What's the matter, Jessie?"

"That book on the patio!" Jessie put her hands to her mouth. "You said it was your grandfather's book, Professor. But it wasn't a gift from your grandfather, was it?" She looked right at him. "It was a book *about* your grandfather!"

"I guess you've found me out," he said, looking around at all the faces staring at him. "My real name's Matthew Cape. I'm Ethan Cape's grandson."

Kate was so startled, she needed a few moments to collect her thoughts. "That would mean . . ."

Matthew nodded. "You and I are second cousins, Kate." The corners of his mouth began to twitch and then he started to laugh. "I came here to add to my collection of photographs, but I've added to my family instead. Thanks to the Aldens," he quickly added.

Benny grinned. "And that's way better than a photograph!"

"You've got that right, Benny," agreed Matthew, who was a changed person now that the truth was out in the open. "I can't thank you kids enough for uncovering the truth about my grandfather. And I'm sorry if I've been a bit . . ." His voice trailed away.

"Unfriendly?" asked Benny.

"Yes, Benny," said Matthew. "I figured if I kept my distance, no one would ask me any personal questions."

"Oh," said Violet, beginning to understand.

"Well, Matthew," Kate said with a twinkle in her eye, "I'm afraid my grandmother's photograph is still off limits. Even to a cousin."

Matthew held up his hands. "That photograph is right where it belongs, Kate."

Lindsay suddenly jumped up. "This calls for a celebration!" She hurried from the room, returning a few moments later with

peanut-butter cookies and milk for everyone.

"Ethan was true to his word," Jessie said, as she reached for a cookie. "He really did come back to see his long-lost sister."

Kate nodded. "I imagine he told my grandmother the truth about their past." She took a long sip of cold milk. "That must have been the secret she wanted to share with the family."

"I guess your great-grandfather had a hunch about that rhyme," said Violet.

"Yes, that would explain why he kept it hidden away," said Kate. "He didn't want to risk losing Sally if it held the truth about the past."

"I knew Thane Pace wasn't a thief," put in Benny. The youngest Alden was all smiles as he took a bite of his cookie. Then his eyes suddenly widened.

"What's wrong?" Jessie asked her little brother in alarm.

Benny answered by reaching into his mouth and pulling out something yellow and blue—it was the bluebird necklace!

"Oh!" cried Lindsay. "How in the world did . . . ?"

Vanessa was clapping her hands. "I bet I know what happened," she said, laughing with relief. "You were making cookies, Lindsay, when you called me to the phone the other day. I remember reaching into the cupboard for a coffee mug. The necklace must've slipped off and landed right in the—"

"Cookie dough!" finished Benny, handing the necklace to Kate.

Kate's smile was dazzling. "What a perfect ending to the evening!" she said, brushing the crumbs from the bluebird charm. "Your grandfather was right—you children really are first-class detectives!"

"Well, one thing's for sure," Henry said with a grin. "Benny really knows how to sink his teeth into a mystery!"

"Especially if it tastes like peanut butter!" said Benny, as he reached for another cookie.